# TITCHY WITCH

and the

# Bully
# Boggarts

For Isobel Louise - welcome
R.I.

To Kath
K.M.

ORCHARD BOOKS
338 Euston Road, London NW1 3BH
*Orchard Books Australia*
Level 17/207 Kent Street, Sydney, NSW 2000
First published in Great Britain in 2003
First paperback publication 2004
This edition published 2008 for Index Books Ltd
ISBN 978 1 40830 194 4
Text © Rose Impey 2003  Illustrations © Katharine McEwen 2003
The rights of Rose Impey to be identified as the author and
Katharine McEwen to be identified as the illustrator of this Work
have been asserted by them in accordance with the
Copyright, Designs and Patents Act, 1988.
A CIP catalogue record for this book is available from the British Library
1 3 5 7 9 10 8 6 4 2
Printed in China

# TITCHY WITCH

### and the

# Bully
# Boggarts

## Rose Impey ★ Katharine McEwen

ORCHARD BOOKS

Titchy-witch

Victor

Eric

Wendel

Weeny-witch

Witchy-witch

Cat-a-bogus

Titchy-witch didn't want to
go to school. She said she had
a tummy-ache.

"Too many Grobble Gums,"
said Cat-a-bogus.

"All little witches have to go to school," said Mum.

"Even this little witch," said Dad.

Titchy-witch wanted Mum to take her to school, but Witchy-witch was too busy with the baby.

So Cat-a-bogus took her instead
and Titchy-witch scowled all
the way.

She didn't want anyone to see her
being taken to school by a cat!
But Gobby-goblin saw her.

When Titchy-witch stuck her nose in the air, the little goblin tripped her up.

So Titchy-witch turned his nose
into a sausage.

It soon turned back, but it still
made him mad.

Gobby-goblin's brother was a
terrible bully.
He stood on Titchy-witch's foot
and twisted her arm behind
her back.

So she turned his head into
a cabbage.

"You wait," said the cabbage.
"After school, we'll get our cousins
onto you. They're boggarts!"

But Titchy-witch didn't even wait
for Cat-a-bogus.
She set off home on her own.

When Titchy-witch was half-way home, she heard a whis-whis-whispering sound.

She knew what it was.
You could smell boggarts a mile
away.

Seven of them jumped out of the bushes. (Boggarts always travel in gangs. They're so stupid they'd get lost on their own.)

Titchy-witch wasn't afraid of one boggart. But seven!

The boggarts called her names:

20

And pulled her hair and pinched her hat.

Smelly-Spelly

They tried to make Titchy-witch cry, but even little witches never cry.

"My dad will turn you all into
toads," she said bravely.
"Let him," croaked the boggarts.

"My mum will turn you all into
pigs," she said.
"Who cares," grunted the boggarts.

Then Titchy-witch had
a great idea.
She made up a spell:

"Pinch of sugar, pinch of spice.
All things pink and sweet and nice.
Turn these boggarts, brown and hairy,
Into little boggart-fairies."

The boggarts stared at each other
and started to squeal.

27

When they saw Cat-a-bogus
coming, the fairy-boggarts
ran away.

Cat-a-bogus told Titchy-witch she was getting too big for her broomstick.

He made her promise she would always wait for him from now on.

Cat-a-bogus was glad she'd learned her lesson, for once.

But Titchy-witch was planning
a little lesson of her own.

# TITCHY WITCH

## Rose Impey ★ Katharine McEwen

Enjoy a little more magic with all the Titchy-witch tales:

All priced at £4.99 each

Colour Crunchies are available from all good
bookshops, or can be ordered direct from the publisher:
Orchard Books, PO BOX 29, Douglas IM99 1BQ
Credit card orders please telephone 01624 836000
or fax 01624 837033
or e-mail: bookshop@enterprise.net for details.

To order please quote title, author and ISBN
and your full name and address.
Cheques and postal orders should be
made payable to 'Bookpost plc'.
Postage and packing is FREE within the UK
(overseas customers should add £1.00 per book).

Prices and availability are subject to change.